Put Beginning Readers on the Right Track with
ALL ABOARD READING™

The All Aboard Reading series is especially ℓ ⋯ ritten by noted authors and illustrated in full colo ⋯ lly want to read—books to excite their imagina ⋯ hem laugh, and support their feelings. With fictic ⋯ igh interest and curriculum-related, All Aboard I ⋯ every young reader. And with four different ⋯ Aboard Reading series lets you choose which books are most ap, ⋯riate for your children and their growing abilities.

Picture Readers
Picture Readers have super-simple texts, with many nouns appearing as rebus pictures. At the end of each book are 24 flash cards—on one side is a rebus picture; on the other side is the written-out word.

Station Stop 1
Station Stop 1 books are best for children who have just begun to read. Simple words and big type make these early reading experiences more comfortable. Picture clues help children to figure out the words on the page. Lots of repetition throughout the text helps children to predict the next word or phrase—an essential step in developing word recognition.

Station Stop 2
Station Stop 2 books are written specifically for children who are reading with help. Short sentences make it easier for early readers to understand what they are reading. Simple plots and simple dialogue help children with reading comprehension.

Station Stop 3
Station Stop 3 books are perfect for children who are reading alone. With longer text and harder words, these books appeal to children who have mastered basic reading skills. More complex stories captivate children who are ready for more challenging books.

In addition to All Aboard Reading books, look for All Aboard Math Readers™ (fiction stories that teach math concepts children are learning in school); All Aboard Science Readers™ (nonfiction books that explore the most fascinating science topics in age-appropriate language); All Aboard Poetry Readers™ (funny, rhyming poems for readers of all levels); and All Aboard Mystery Readers™ (puzzling tales where children piece together evidence with the characters).

All Aboard for happy reading!

Visit www.strawberryshortcake.com to join the Friendship Club and redeem your Strawberry Shortcake Berry Points for "berry" fun stuff!

GROSSET & DUNLAP
Published by the Penguin Group
Penguin Group (USA) Inc., 375 Hudson Street, New York, New York 10014, U.S.A.
Penguin Group (Canada), 10 Alcorn Avenue, Toronto, Ontario, Canada M4V 3B2
(a division of Pearson Penguin Canada Inc.)
Penguin Books Ltd, 80 Strand, London WC2R 0RL, England
Penguin Ireland, 25 St Stephen's Green, Dublin 2, Ireland
(a division of Penguin Books Ltd)
Penguin Group (Australia), 250 Camberwell Road, Camberwell, Victoria 3124, Australia
(a division of Pearson Australia Group Pty Ltd)
Penguin Books India Pvt Ltd, 11 Community Centre, Panchsheel Park,
New Delhi - 110 017, India
Penguin Group (NZ), Cnr Airborne and Rosedale Roads, Albany, Auckland 1310, New Zealand
(a division of Pearson New Zealand Ltd)
Penguin Books (South Africa) (Pty) Ltd, 24 Sturdee Avenue, Rosebank,
Johannesburg 2196, South Africa

Penguin Books Ltd, Registered Offices:
80 Strand, London WC2R 0RL, England

Strawberry Shortcake™ © 2005 by Those Characters From Cleveland, Inc. Used under license by Penguin Young Readers Group. All rights reserved. Published by Grosset & Dunlap, a division of Penguin Young Readers Group, 345 Hudson Street, New York, New York 10014. ALL ABOARD READING and GROSSET & DUNLAP are trademarks of Penguin Group (USA) Inc. Printed in the U.S.A.

Library of Congress Control Number: 2004017189

ISBN 0-448-43848-8   10 9 8 7 6 5

Strawberry Shortcake's Show-and-Tell Surprise

By Megan E. Bryant

Illustrated by Scott Neely

Grosset & Dunlap

Strawberry Shortcake
loves school.
School is berry fun!

Strawberry Shortcake
loves show-and-tell the best.
And tomorrow is
show-and-tell day!

Strawberry wants to show
something berry special.
What should she bring?

A book?

Too heavy.

A pencil?
Too tiny.

A painting?
Too messy.

9

A ball?

Too bouncy.

Strawberry Shortcake
doesn't know
<u>what</u> to bring
for show-and-tell!

After school,
Strawberry Shortcake
walks home.
It is berry windy.

What's that?

It is a bird's nest!

There are no
mama birds around.
There are no
papa birds around.
Who will take care of the egg?

Strawberry Shortcake will!

Strawberry Shortcake
takes the nest home.
She keeps the egg warm.
She keeps the egg safe.

Then Strawberry has
a berry good idea.
She can bring the nest to school
for show-and-tell!

Before school,
Strawberry Shortcake
puts the nest in a box.
She walks to school
berry carefully.

Strawberry waits and waits.

At last,

it is time for show-and-tell.

Orange Blossom shows a plant.

Huckleberry Pie shows a toy car.

Blueberry Muffin shows
a picture.

Angel Cake shows a cake.

Ginger Snap shows
some cookie cutters.

Then it is
Strawberry Shortcake's turn.
She is berry excited!

Strawberry Shortcake
opens the box.
But where is the egg?

Surprise!

The egg hatched!

Now it is a baby bird!

The baby bird is berry cute.

But it needs a mama bird
to take care of it.

The kids go outside.

They put the nest back

in the tree.

The mama bird
flies home!

What a berry special
show-and-tell surprise!